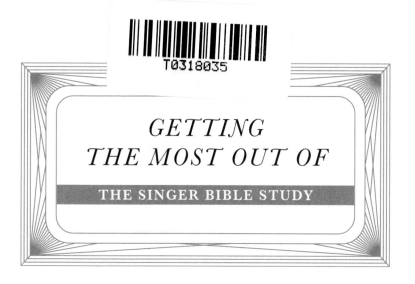

GETTING THE MOST OUT OF

THE SINGER BIBLE STUDY

KNOWING CHRIST is where faith begins. From there we are shaped through the essentials of discipleship: Bible study, prayer, Christian community, worship, and much more. We learn to grow in Christlike character, pursue justice, and share our faith with others. We persevere through doubts and gain wisdom for daily life. These are the topics woven into the IVP Signature Bible Studies. Working through this series will help you practice the essentials by exploring biblical truths found in classic books.

HOW IT'S PUT TOGETHER

Each session includes an opening quotation and suggested reading from the book *The Singer*, a session goal to help guide your study, reflection questions to stir your thoughts on the topic, the text of the Bible passage, questions for exploring the passage, response questions to help you apply what you've learned, and a closing suggestion for prayer.

The workbook format is ideal for personal study and also allows group members to prepare in advance for discussions and record discussion notes. The responses you write here can form a permanent record of your thoughts and spiritual progress.

Throughout the guide are study-note sidebars that may be useful for group leaders or individuals. These notes do not give the answers, but they do provide additional background information on certain questions and can challenge participants to think deeper or differently about the content.

WHAT KIND OF GUIDE IS THIS?

The studies are not designed to merely tell you what one person thinks. Instead, through inductive study they will help you discover for yourself what Scripture is saying. Each study deals with a particular passage—rather than jumping around the Bible—so that you can really delve into the biblical author's meaning in that context.

The studies ask three different kinds of questions about the Bible passage:

✳ *Observation* questions help you to understand the content of the passage by asking about the basic facts: who, what, when, where, and how.

✳ *Interpretation* questions delve into the meaning of the passage.

✳ *Application* questions help you discover implications for growing in Christ in your own life.

These three keys unlock the treasures of the biblical writings and help you live them out.

This is a thought-provoking guide. Each question assumes a variety of answers. Many questions do not have "right" answers, particularly questions that aim at meaning or application. Instead, the questions should inspire readers to explore the passage more thoroughly.

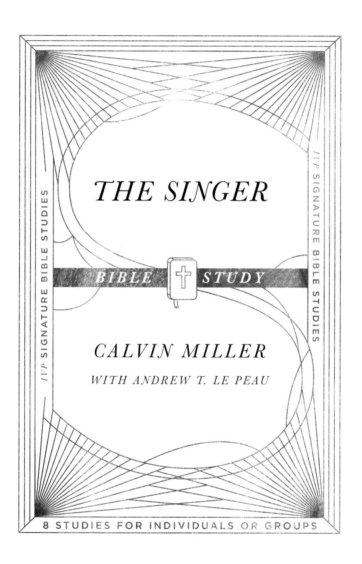

THE SINGER

BIBLE ✝ STUDY

IVP SIGNATURE BIBLE STUDIES

CALVIN MILLER

WITH ANDREW T. LE PEAU

8 STUDIES FOR INDIVIDUALS OR GROUPS

An imprint of InterVarsity Press
Downers Grove, Illinois

InterVarsity Press
P.O. Box 1400, Downers Grove, IL 60515-1426
ivpress.com
email@ivpress.com

This study guide adapts material from The Singer, *25th anniversary edition ©2001 by Calvin Miller, first edition ©1975 by InterVarsity Christian Fellowship® of the United States of America.*

InterVarsity Press® is the book-publishing division of InterVarsity Christian Fellowship/USA®, a movement of students and faculty active on campus at hundreds of universities, colleges, and schools of nursing in the United States of America, and a member movement of the International Fellowship of Evangelical Students. For information about local and regional activities, visit intervarsity.org.

All Scripture quotations, unless otherwise indicated, are taken from The Holy Bible, New International Version®, NIV®. Copyright © 1973, 1978, 1984, 2011 by Biblica, Inc.™ Used by permission of Zondervan. All rights reserved worldwide. www.zondervan.com. The "NIV" and "New International Version" are trademarks registered in the United States Patent and Trademark Office by Biblica, Inc.™

Cover design and image composite: Autumn Short
Interior design: Daniel van Loon
Images: abstract aluminum background © oxygen / Moment Collection / Getty Images
        tree illustration © CSA Images / Getty Images
        glittering gold background © MirageC / Moment Collection / Getty Images

ISBN 978-0-8308-4842-3 (print)
ISBN 978-0-8308-4925-3 (digital)

Printed in the United States of America ♾

InterVarsity Press is committed to ecological stewardship and to the conservation of natural resources in all our operations. This book was printed using sustainably sourced paper.

P	20	19	18	17	16	15	14	13	12	11	10	9	8	7	6	5	4	3	2	1
Y	37	36	35	34	33	32	31	30	29	28	27	26	25	24	23	22	21	20		

CONTENTS

This study guide is flexible. You can use it for individual study, but it is also great for a variety of groups—student, professional, neighborhood, or church groups. Each study takes about forty-five minutes in a group setting or thirty minutes in personal study.

SUGGESTIONS FOR INDIVIDUAL STUDY

1. This guide is based on a classic book that will enrich your spiritual life. If you have not read *The Singer,* you may want to read the portion recommended in the "Read" section before you begin your study. The ideas in the book will enhance your study, but the Bible text will be the focus of each session.

2. Begin each session with prayer, asking God to speak to you from his Word about this particular topic.

3. As you read the Scripture passage, reproduced for you from the New International Version, you may wish to mark phrases that seem important. Note in the margin any questions that come to your mind.

4. Close with the suggested prayer found at the end of each session. Speak to God about insights you have gained. Tell him of any desires you have for specific growth. Ask him to help you attempt to live out the principles described in that passage. You may wish to write your own prayer in this guide or a journal.

SUGGESTIONS FOR GROUP MEMBERS

Joining a Bible study group can be a great avenue to spiritual growth. Here are a few guidelines that will help you as you participate in the studies in this guide.

1. Reading the recommended portion of *The Singer,* before or after each session, will enhance your study and understanding of the themes in this guide.

2. These studies use methods of inductive Bible study, which focuses on a particular passage of Scripture and works on it in depth. So try to dive into the given text instead of referring to other Scripture passages.

3. Questions are designed to help a group discuss together a passage of Scripture in order to understand its content, meaning, and implications. Most people are either natural talkers or natural listeners, yet this type of study works best if all members participate more or less evenly. Try to curb any natural tendency toward either excessive talking or excessive quiet. You and the rest of the group will benefit!

4. Most questions in this guide allow for a variety of answers. If you disagree with someone else's comment, gently say so. Then explain your own point of view from the passage before you.

5. Be willing to lead a discussion, if asked. Much of the preparation for leading has already been accomplished in the writing of this guide.

6. Respect the privacy of people in your group. Many people share things within the context of a Bible study group that they do not want to be public knowledge. Assume that personal information spoken within the group setting is private, unless you are specifically told otherwise.

7. We recommend that all groups agree on a few basic guidelines. You may wish to adapt this list to your situation:

   a. Anything said in this group is considered confidential and will not be discussed outside the group unless specific permission is given to do so.

   b. We will provide time for each person present to talk if he or she feels comfortable doing so.

c. We will talk about ourselves and our own situations, avoiding conversation about other people.

d. We will listen attentively to each other.

e. We will pray for each other.

8. Enjoy your study. Prepare to grow!

SUGGESTIONS FOR GROUP LEADERS

There are specific suggestions to help you in the "Leading a Small Group" section. It describes how to lead a group discussion, gives helpful tips on group dynamics, and suggests ways to deal with problems that may arise during the discussion. With such helps, someone with little or no experience can lead an effective group study. Read this section carefully, even if you are leading only one group meeting.

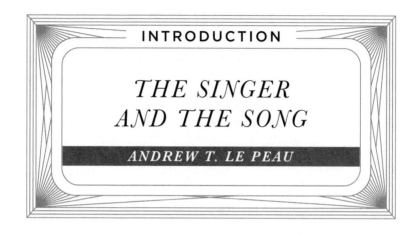

THE SINGER AND THE SONG

ANDREW T. LE PEAU

ONE SLEEPLESS NIGHT, Calvin Miller awoke and a song was there; but more than that, the Singer was there. So Miller began to write what became the bestselling mythic retelling of the old, old story—*The Singer*.

When *Godspell* and *Jesus Christ Superstar* where introduced on Broadway in the 1970s, Miller had thought someone ought to create a portrayal of Jesus that the Gospel writers themselves might recognize. He hesitated, though, at such an audacious task. But his late-night stirrings continued, and so did he.

The poetic story of a troubadour roused to sing the Ancient Star-Song resonated with hundreds of thousands of readers. The cast of characters the Singer encountered were also familiar . . . and yet new.

A River Singer, who confirmed the calling. A World Hater, who seductively sought to stop the Singer at every step. The Friendship Seller, who ceased selling love only to end up owing it everything. A Madman made to dance at the World Hater's incessant piping. And finally, the Keepers of the Ancient Ways, who turned the song of life into a dirge of death.

In this Bible study guide we meet these characters and the Gospel stories they sprang from. An excerpt from *The Singer* introduces each session, but you are also encouraged to read the chapters from *The Singer* that are noted. In this way, you will progress through the whole book in the course of this guide.

Joe DeVelasco's evocative line drawings were an integral part of the appeal of *The Singer*. They powerfully convey the drama and emotion that brought fresh perspective to well-known stories. You may want to look up the corresponding image in *The Singer* as you reflect on each excerpt.

While I did not work with Calvin Miller as his editor for *The Singer,* I had the privilege of doing so on many of his subsequent books. Calvin, who died in 2012, always had a quiet joy about him that was infectious. I also found him to be passionate about words, about stories, and about the Lord he loved all his life. May the same be so for you.

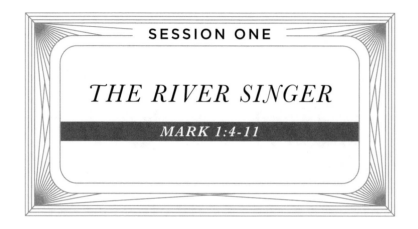

And there where water lapped at his fatigue, he heard a singer, singing his compelling carols to the empty air.

The tradesman knew that it was just an earth song, for it was different from the Star-Song which begged him be its singer—yet somehow like it.

The River Singer finished and they walked into the trees.

"Are you the Troubadour, who knows the Ancient Star-Song?" the tradesman softly asked.

"No, *you* are the Great Troubadour for whom the songless world, so long has waited," the River Singer said. "Sing, for many years now, I have hungered to hear the Ancient Star-Song . . ."

"I am a tradesman only . . ."

Then the River Singer waded out into the water and beckoned with his hand. Slowly the tradesman followed. . . .

The water swirled around them and the music surged.

Every chord seemed to fuse the world in oneness. . . .

Then over that thin silver stream the thunder pealed, and a
voice called from the sky above . . .

> "Tradesman! You are the Troubadour! Go now
>   and sing!"

SESSION GOAL	READING
To respond to God's call to confession and living by his Spirit.	Chapters I–III of *The Singer*

REFLECT

* Think of a time you were involved in launching a new initiative at home, school, work, church, or in your community. Describe how you felt.

* When you're starting something new, what can help it launch successfully?

STUDY

READ MARK 1:4-11.

⁴John the Baptist appeared in the wilderness, preaching a
baptism of repentance for the forgiveness of sins. ⁵The
whole Judean countryside and all the people of Jerusalem
went out to him. Confessing their sins, they were baptized
by him in the Jordan River. ⁶John wore clothing made of
camel's hair, with a leather belt around his waist, and he ate

locusts and wild honey. ⁷And this was his message: "After me comes the one more powerful than I, the straps of whose sandals I am not worthy to stoop down and untie. ⁸I baptize you with water, but he will baptize you with the Holy Spirit."

⁹At that time Jesus came from Nazareth in Galilee and was baptized by John in the Jordan. ¹⁰Just as Jesus was coming up out of the water, he saw heaven being torn open and the Spirit descending on him like a dove. ¹¹And a voice came from heaven: "You are my Son, whom I love; with you I am well pleased."

1. John had two messages for the people. What were they?

2. How were the two messages connected?

3. Why is confession needed both personally and as a nation?

The Jews were under the rule of Rome during this time. Many assumed they were occupied by a foreign power because God was punishing the nation for their sins—not just personally but also corporately. Like Daniel and Nehemiah, who centuries before confessed the sins of the nation during exile, many came to John to do the same.

4. How would the ministry of the person coming after John be different?

5. Christians have many ideas about the Holy Spirit. Focusing *only* on what is in this passage, what do we learn about the Spirit?

> John's seemingly odd attire of camel hair and leather belt (Mark 1:6) recall the prophet Elijah, who is described similarly (2 Kings 1:8). Regarding John's diet, Elijah was also instructed to live off the provisions God would supply (1 Kings 17:2-6).

6. When Jesus was baptized, three things happened. What were they, and what is the significance of each?

> Isaiah 64:1 uses the language of tearing the heavens in the context of God coming down to save his people from their enemies.

7. How would all this have confirmed Jesus' mission, for him and possibly for others?

RESPOND

✳ Why might people today need to confess not just personal sins but also sins of an organization, community, or nation?

✳ God desires more from us than just confessing sins. What else does God desire?

PRAY

Father, Son, and Spirit, we come to you knowing we have failed to follow your ways in thought, word, and deed. We ask that you will forgive us individually and corporately. More than that, we ask for the grace and power of the Spirit to love you and to love others this day and this week. In your holy triune name we pray. Amen.

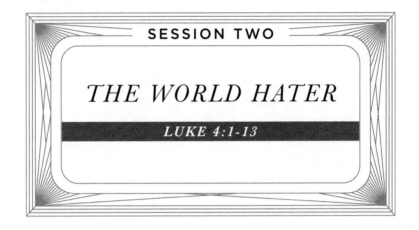

"Hello, Singer!"

"Hello, World Hater," the Troubadour responded.

"You know my name, old friend of man?"

"As you know mine, old enemy of God."

"What brings you to the desert?"

"The Giver of the Song!" . . .

"Now," cried the World Hater, "Let's do this tune at once. I'll pipe, you sing. Think of the thousand kingdoms that will dance about our feet."

"No, Hater, I'll not sing your melodies," the Troubadour replied.

"What then Singer will you sing?"

"The Ancient Star-Song of the Father-Spirit."

"Alone, without accompaniment?"

"Yes, Hater, all alone if need be."

"You need my pipe, man."

"You need my song instead."

"The music of your song is far beyond my tiny pipe."

"Then, go! For I shall never sing a lesser piece."

SESSION GOAL	READING
To respond to temptation following the pattern Jesus set.	Chapters IV–V of *The Singer*

REFLECT

✳ What has been your experience in reading or studying the Bible?

✳ What difficulties do you have when you read and study Scripture?

STUDY

READ LUKE 4:1-13.

¹Jesus, full of the Holy Spirit, left the Jordan and was led by the Spirit into the wilderness, ²where for forty days he was tempted by the devil. He ate nothing during those days, and at the end of them he was hungry.

³The devil said to him, "If you are the Son of God, tell this stone to become bread."

⁴Jesus answered, "It is written: 'Man shall not live on bread alone.'"

⁵The devil led him up to a high place and showed him in an instant all the kingdoms of the world. ⁶And he said to him, "I will give you all their authority and splendor; it has been given to me, and I can give it to anyone I want to. ⁷If you worship me, it will all be yours."

⁸Jesus answered, "It is written: 'Worship the Lord your God and serve him only.'"

⁹The devil led him to Jerusalem and had him stand on the highest point of the temple. "If you are the Son of God," he said, "throw yourself down from here. ¹⁰For it is written:

"'He will command his angels concerning you
        to guard you carefully;
¹¹they will lift you up in their hands,
        so that you will not strike your foot against a stone.'"

¹²Jesus answered, "It is said: 'Do not put the Lord your God to the test.'"

¹³When the devil had finished all this tempting, he left him until an opportune time.

1. In Luke 4:1-2, what are the different dynamics at work in this situation and in Jesus?

2. Look at the three challenges the devil presents. Give one word to summarize each.

3. Jesus responds to the devil with three passages from Deuteronomy. The first is Deuteronomy 8:1-3. What is the significance of the parallels between that passage and what we read in Luke?

Why would Jesus focus on the book of Deuteronomy? In that Old Testament book Israel is still in the wilderness but on the verge of entering the Promised Land. Here Moses gives several speeches that look back and look forward. He notes how Israel was rescued from Egypt but failed often to meet the challenges it faced in the wilderness, falling to idolatry and failing to trust God to provide. He then urges Israel to obey the Lord.

4. The second challenge may seem empty. After all, isn't Jesus already ruler of all the kingdoms of the world? But to instantly (almost effortlessly) be given this authority was not the way Jesus was ultimately to be acknowledged as king. What instead was God's plan for how this would happen?

5. Why would the devil's proposal then be potentially tempting to Jesus?

The last two passages Jesus mentions are from Deuteronomy 6. Here we find the famous Shema (vv. 4-5), which ancient Israelites were to repeat daily. Deuteronomy 6:16 references Massah. That's where the Israelites complained about having no water in the desert soon after God had miraculously brought them out of slavery (Exodus 17:1-7).

6. In the last test, the devil himself quotes Scripture—Psalm 91:11-12, a wonderful psalm about the safety we can find in God. What are ways we can also misuse or misinterpret Scripture?

7. Why do you think the devil twice uses the phrase, "If you are the Son of God"?

RESPOND

❋ How can doubts about God and his promises set the stage for the temptations we face?

❋ We are whole people—body, soul, and spirit. Just as Jesus was potentially more susceptible to temptation when he was physically weak and hungry, how can a weakened physical and emotional state make us more susceptible as well?

PRAY

Our Father, give us this day our daily bread, and lead us not into temptation but deliver us from evil. For thine is the kingdom, the power, and the glory forever. Amen.

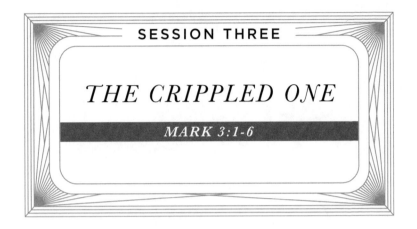

THE CRIPPLED ONE

MARK 3:1-6

The Singer stopped. Beside the road he saw a brown-eyed child. Her mouth was drawn in hard, firm lines that could not bend to either smile or frown. Her sickness ate her spirit, devouring all the sparkle in her eyes.

Her legs misshapen as they were, lay useless underneath the coarsest sort of cloth. The Singer knelt beside her in the dust and touched her limpid hand and cried. He drew the cloth away that hid her legs. He reached his calloused hand and touched the small, misshapen foot. . . .

Above them towered the World Hater.

"I knew you'd come," he said. "You will, of course, make straight her twisted limbs?"

"I will, World Hater . . . but can you have no mercy? She's but a child. Can her wholeness menace you in any way? Would it so embarrass you to see her skipping in the sun? Why hate such little, suffering life?"

"Why chide me, Singer? She's Earthmaker's awful error. Tell your Father-Spirit he should take more time when he creates."

"No, it is love which brings a thousand children into life in health. It is hate that cripples each exception to eternal joy. But why must you forever toy with nature to make yourself such ugly pastimes of delight?" . . .

The Singer scooped the frightened child into his arms. He sang and set her in the sunny fields and thrilled to watch her run.

SESSION GOAL	READING
To commit to live in a way that honors doing good over following rules.	Chapters VI–IX of *The Singer*

REFLECT

✳ What do you think are the most important commands in Christianity and why?

STUDY

READ MARK 3:1-6.

[1]Another time Jesus went into the synagogue, and a man with a shriveled hand was there. [2]Some of them were looking for a reason to accuse Jesus, so they watched him closely to see if he would heal him on the Sabbath. [3]Jesus said to the man with the shriveled hand, "Stand up in front of everyone."

⁴Then Jesus asked them, "Which is lawful on the Sabbath: to do good or to do evil, to save life or to kill?" But they remained silent.

⁵He looked around at them in anger and, deeply distressed at their stubborn hearts, said to the man, "Stretch out your hand." He stretched it out, and his hand was completely restored. ⁶Then the Pharisees went out and began to plot with the Herodians how they might kill Jesus.

1. What conflict is brewing in this passage?

2. Why does Jesus make such a public issue about healing when he knows some are looking for an excuse to make accusations against him?

3. What point is Jesus trying to make in his question about the Sabbath?

Healing would have been considered a kind of work and so, presumably, forbidden on the Sabbath, the day of rest. Nonetheless, "healing by speaking is not a breach of the Sabbath. He prepares no ointments or potions and lifts nothing. Jesus only violates the Pharisees' finespun interpretation of the law."*

4. Why is this question effective in silencing the Pharisees?

5. Why does Jesus become upset with his accusers (Mark 3:5)?

> In verse 4 Jesus alludes to Moses' final exhortation to Israel: "I call heaven and earth to witness against you today, that I have set before you life and death, blessing and curse. Therefore choose life" (Deuteronomy 30:19 ESV). Jesus suggests that the force of the whole of Old Testament law supports his action.

6. Who in this episode ultimately affirms the Sabbath and who violates it? How?

7. The Pharisees thought the government was the problem—Roman rule. How does the excerpt from *The Singer* offer another perspective?

✴ RESPOND

✴ How does a commitment to rules sometimes lead Christians to oppose helping people in need?

✴ How can we keep a proper balance in honoring the Sabbath?

✴ PRAY

Father, Son, and Spirit, we thank you that you are always on the side of life, that you desire every human to flourish body, soul, and spirit. May you grant us compassion for those who are homeless, for refugees, for the sick, for the mentally and emotionally disabled, for those who are far from you. May we always remember that loving you and loving others fulfills the whole law. So be it.

*David E. Garland, *Mark*, NIVAC (Grand Rapids, MI: Zondervan, 1996), 109.

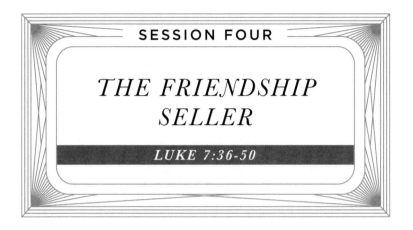

He met a woman in the street. She leaned against an open door and sang through her half-parted lips a song that he could barely hear. He knew her friendship was for hire. She was without a doubt a study in desire. Her hair fell free around her shoulders. And intrigue played upon her lips.

"Are you betrothed?" she asked.

"No, only loved," he answered.

"And do you pay for love?"

"No, but I owe it everything...."

"We sometimes give ourselves to hate in masquerade and only think it love. And all our lives we sing the song we thought was right. The Canyon of the Damned is filled with singers who thought they knew a love song ... Listen while I sing for you a song of love."

He began the melody so vital to the dying men around him. "In the beginning was the song of love ..."

She listened and knew for the first time she was hearing all
of love there was. Her eyes swam when he finished. She
sobbed and sobbed in shame. "Forgive me, Father-Spirit, for
I am sinful and undone . . . for singing weary years of all the
wrong words . . ."

He left her in the street and walked away, and as he left he
heard her singing his new song.

SESSION GOAL	**READING**
To live increasingly as those who've been forgiven.	Chapters X–XI of *The Singer*

 **REFLECT**

✳ Describe a time you misjudged someone when you first met.

✳ Why do we tend to give more respect to prominent people and
leaders than to people with less money or accomplishments?

STUDY

READ LUKE 7:36-50.

³⁶When one of the Pharisees invited Jesus to have dinner with him, he went to the Pharisee's house and reclined at the table. ³⁷A woman in that town who lived a sinful life learned that Jesus was eating at the Pharisee's house, so she came there with an alabaster jar of perfume. ³⁸As she stood behind him at his feet weeping, she began to wet his feet with her tears. Then she wiped them with her hair, kissed them and poured perfume on them.

³⁹When the Pharisee who had invited him saw this, he said to himself, "If this man were a prophet, he would know who is touching him and what kind of woman she is—that she is a sinner."

⁴⁰Jesus answered him, "Simon, I have something to tell you."

"Tell me, teacher," he said.

⁴¹"Two people owed money to a certain moneylender. One owed him five hundred denarii, and the other fifty. ⁴²Neither of them had the money to pay him back, so he forgave the debts of both. Now which of them will love him more?"

⁴³Simon replied, "I suppose the one who had the bigger debt forgiven."

"You have judged correctly," Jesus said.

⁴⁴Then he turned toward the woman and said to Simon, "Do you see this woman? I came into your house. You did not give me any water for my feet, but she wet my feet with her tears and wiped them with her hair. ⁴⁵You did not give me a kiss, but this woman, from the time I entered, has not

stopped kissing my feet. ⁴⁶You did not put oil on my head, but she has poured perfume on my feet. ⁴⁷Therefore, I tell you, her many sins have been forgiven—as her great love has shown. But whoever has been forgiven little loves little."

⁴⁸Then Jesus said to her, "Your sins are forgiven."

⁴⁹The other guests began to say among themselves, "Who is this who even forgives sins?"

⁵⁰Jesus said to the woman, "Your faith has saved you; go in peace."

1. Describe what is happening in the first verses of this story (36-38).

> A large dinner party of this sort would likely have been a semi-public, semi-open-air event. Instead of sitting in chairs, the guests recline on pillows, facing a long, low table with food on it, with their feet pointed outward. Thus an uninvited woman could show up and clean Jesus' feet.

2. Looking at verse 39, why does Simon react in this way?

3. What is Jesus' point about the two debtors?

Since most streets were dirt roads, when guests entered a home, it was common courtesy for hosts to provide water to remove the day's grime (see Genesis 18:4). A hearty Middle Eastern kiss and oil for a dry face (Psalm 23:5) would also have been customary for guests.

4. In what ways does Jesus then compare the woman with Simon (vv. 44-47)?

5. Do you think Simon intentionally slighted Jesus, or was it an oversight? Explain.

6. Why is love a proper response to having been forgiven?

7. Does Simon need to be forgiven much or little? Explain.

> The temple is where Jews would normally receive
> forgiveness, after having offered a sacrifice. The
> guests are startled because Jesus assumes
> the authority to offer forgiveness outside the
> temple context and without being a priest.

RESPOND

✳ Why is it sometimes harder for religious people to respond in love to God and others?

✳ Consider whether you feel you've been forgiven much or little by God. How have you responded as a result?

PRAY

Our Father, forgive us our sins, as we have forgiven those who have sinned against us. May we know deeply how you have forgiven us and as a result may we live lives of loving gratitude to you and others. Amen.

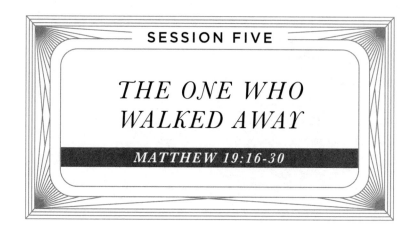

The Miller who was still at work seemed most determined to finish out his toil by starlight. It was only by the merest chance he found the Singer sleeping by the stream just above the giant wheel....

The Singer was about to ask him where he found the mason to quarry such impressive stones, when suddenly he discovered that one of the Miller's hands was badly scarred and crippled....

"I will," observed the Singer, "make it useful once again if you will desire it whole and believe it can be."

"It cannot be so easy, Singer. Would you wave your magic wand above such suffering and have it all be done with?"...

"I have no pain like yours, but I have a healing melody. Earthmaker gave the song to me for healing hands like yours."...

"Oh that such healing now were possible—the speed I might regain in working at the mill. But no, it cannot be. Can you not understand? Have you no sympathy for suffering? Are you so empty of conscience as to suggest a hopeless remedy?"...

He waited for the Singer to join him in his pity, but when he
raised his head for understanding, the door stood open on the
night and the Singer was nowhere to be seen.

SESSION GOAL	READING
To be open to the full range of good things God has in mind for us.	Chapters XII-XIII of *The Singer*

 **REFLECT**

＊ Why do you think the Miller refused healing from the Singer?

＊ If someone came to you and asked how to gain eternal life,
what would you say?

 **STUDY**

READ MATTHEW 19:16-30.

[16]Just then a man came up to Jesus and asked, "Teacher,
what good thing must I do to get eternal life?"

[17]"Why do you ask me about what is good?" Jesus replied. "There is only One who is good. If you want to enter
life, keep the commandments."

¹⁸"Which ones?" he inquired.

Jesus replied, "'You shall not murder, you shall not commit adultery, you shall not steal, you shall not give false testimony, ¹⁹honor your father and mother,' and 'love your neighbor as yourself.'"

²⁰"All these I have kept," the young man said. "What do I still lack?"

²¹Jesus answered, "If you want to be perfect, go, sell your possessions and give to the poor, and you will have treasure in heaven. Then come, follow me."

²²When the young man heard this, he went away sad, because he had great wealth.

²³Then Jesus said to his disciples, "Truly I tell you, it is hard for someone who is rich to enter the kingdom of heaven. ²⁴Again I tell you, it is easier for a camel to go through the eye of a needle than for someone who is rich to enter the kingdom of God."

²⁵When the disciples heard this, they were greatly astonished and asked, "Who then can be saved?"

²⁶Jesus looked at them and said, "With man this is impossible, but with God all things are possible."

²⁷Peter answered him, "We have left everything to follow you! What then will there be for us?"

²⁸Jesus said to them, "Truly I tell you, at the renewal of all things, when the Son of Man sits on his glorious throne, you who have followed me will also sit on twelve thrones, judging the twelve tribes of Israel. ²⁹And everyone who has left houses or brothers or sisters or father or mother or wife or children or fields for my sake will receive a hundred times as much and will inherit eternal life. ³⁰But many who are first will be last, and many who are last will be first."

1. What is Jesus' point in responding to the man, "There is only One who is good"?

2. Look at Exodus 20:2-17. What commands does Jesus not include in his list, and why does he skip them?

3. Jesus has just said no one is good except God. What is ironic then about the young man's response in verse 20?

4. In verse 21, why does Jesus give such a challenging response to the man?

5. Why is money so often a barrier to our relationship with God?

> Caring for the poor, the oppressed, orphans, and widows is a sign of righteousness (Job 29:12, 16; 31:16-22; Psalm 41:1; Proverbs 14:21; 29:7; Zechariah 7:9-10). God also exhibits particular concern for those in need (Deuteronomy 10:18-19; Psalm 146:5-9).

6. What good things does Jesus say that God gives to those who commit their lives to him?

According to Proverbs, riches can be a blessing from God (Proverbs 3:16; 8:18). At the same time, Proverbs warns against focusing one's life on getting rich because wealth can come quickly and be gone just as quickly (Proverbs 23:4-5; 27:24; 28:20, 22). Psalms 39:5-6; 49:5-6, 10, 16-17; 52:6-7; 62:10 say much the same thing.

 **RESPOND**

✳ Why do you think Jesus' answer to the question about eternal life might differ from ours?

✳ Why do we sometimes turn down the good things God has to offer us?

 **PRAY**

Jesus, you are Lord of every aspect of our lives. Give us insight to see where we are holding back and peace to open our hands to receive from you, for the sake of you and your kingdom. Amen.

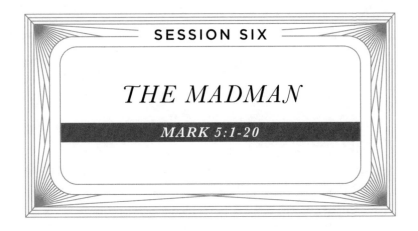

THE MADMAN

MARK 5:1-20

A heavy set of chains hung from a great foundation stone that held the towering wall. Manacles hung bolted on the wrists of a burly, naked man. . . .

"Is he mad?" the Singer asked.

"Senselessly," the Hater answered.

"Who brings him bread and water?"

"I do."

"Why?"

"To see him dance in madness without a tiny hope! Imagine my delight when he raves and screams in chains. Would you like for me to wake this animal?"

"He is a man. Earthmaker made him so. What is his name?"

"The Crowd."

"Why such a name?"

"Because within this sleeping hulk there are a thousand hating spirits from the Canyon of the Damned. They leap at him with sounds no ears but his can hear. They dive at him with screaming lights no other eyes can see. And in his torment he will hold his shaggy head and whimper. Then he rises and strains in fury against the chains to tear them from the wall. Stand back and see."

SESSION GOAL	**READING**
To respond with faith in the face of fear.	Chapters XIV-XV of *The Singer*

 **REFLECT**

* What encourages your faith?

* What tends to make you nervous or afraid?

 **STUDY**

READ MARK 5:1-20.

¹They went across the lake to the region of the Gerasenes. ²When Jesus got out of the boat, a man with an impure spirit came from the tombs to meet him. ³This man lived

in the tombs, and no one could bind him anymore, not even with a chain. ⁴For he had often been chained hand and foot, but he tore the chains apart and broke the irons on his feet. No one was strong enough to subdue him. ⁵Night and day among the tombs and in the hills he would cry out and cut himself with stones.

⁶When he saw Jesus from a distance, he ran and fell on his knees in front of him. ⁷He shouted at the top of his voice, "What do you want with me, Jesus, Son of the Most High God? In God's name don't torture me!" ⁸For Jesus had said to him, "Come out of this man, you impure spirit!"

⁹Then Jesus asked him, "What is your name?"

"My name is Legion," he replied, "for we are many." ¹⁰And he begged Jesus again and again not to send them out of the area.

¹¹A large herd of pigs was feeding on the nearby hillside. ¹²The demons begged Jesus, "Send us among the pigs; allow us to go into them." ¹³He gave them permission, and the impure spirits came out and went into the pigs. The herd, about two thousand in number, rushed down the steep bank into the lake and were drowned.

¹⁴Those tending the pigs ran off and reported this in the town and countryside, and the people went out to see what had happened. ¹⁵When they came to Jesus, they saw the man who had been possessed by the legion of demons, sitting there, dressed and in his right mind; and they were afraid. ¹⁶Those who had seen it told the people what had happened to the demon-possessed man—and told about the pigs as well. ¹⁷Then the people began to plead with Jesus to leave their region.

¹⁸As Jesus was getting into the boat, the man who had been demon-possessed begged to go with him. ¹⁹Jesus did not let him, but said, "Go home to your own people and tell them how much the Lord has done for you, and how he has had mercy on you." ²⁰So the man went away and began to tell in the Decapolis how much Jesus had done for him. And all the people were amazed.

1. In what ways do you see power conflicts at work in the whole passage?

2. In the ancient world one was thought to be able to control spiritual beings by using their names. How do both Legion and Jesus seem to employ this strategy?

3. How does Jesus respond to the requests that three different parties make of him in this passage?

A legion was a Roman military unit consisting of five to six thousand troops. That may not represent the exact number of demons present but certainly communicates a very large number.

Was Jesus wrong to destroy the pigs? First, Jesus did not kill the pigs. The demons did. Second, Jesus is not said to know all things (see Mark 13:32) and may not have known what the demons would do. Third, while property was destroyed, the man was restored. And people are of more value than things. In addition, Jews would have seen the sea (a source of chaos, evil, and opposition to God; for example, Psalm 89:9-10, Isaiah 27:1, and Daniel 7:2-3) as an appropriate place for unclean pigs and demons to end up.

4. Why do you think he responds in these ways?

5. How do you see the themes of fear and faith play out in the various characters in this story?

6. In Mark 5:19-20, what is the difference between what Jesus told the man to do and what he actually did?

RESPOND

✳ We all react to those we think might be our enemies. In this passage lots of potential enemies are presented—the man who is possessed, Gentiles, maybe Roman soldiers and the Roman government, the townspeople. Even Jesus is considered a threat by some. But none of these are true enemies. Instead, Satan and his demons are. Why is that an important perspective to remember?

✳ How can Jesus help you to respond in faith when confronted by your fears?

PRAY

Heavenly Lord and Shepherd, you know our fears. Help us to see how you meet our needs, give us rest, provide us with refreshment, renew our souls, and protect us even in the darkest of times. You provide abundantly for us and sustain us with your faithful presence. Thank you. Amen.

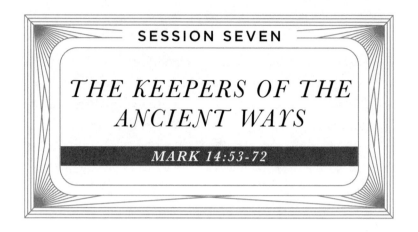

"Is it true? Are you the Troubadour? Can you sing the Ancient Star-Song?"

"I am he. I know the song."

"Then sing it now," agreed the Keepers of the Ancient Ways. . . .

> The Shrine of older days must be laid by.
> Mankind must see Earthmaker left the sky.
> And he is with us. They must concede that
> I am he. They must believe the Song or die. . . .

"Liar!" they cried again. "Strike him on the mouth." A bearded monk, who only lately read the liturgy, laid aside his scroll and struck the Singer on the mouth. The blood ran down his chin.

"Listen, men of Terra!" cried the Grand Musician. "He sings a lie. Earthmaker loves the Shrine. He has loved it for a thousand holidays."

The Singer stumbled to his feet and cried above the crowd. "Earthmaker loves neither shrines nor holidays. He loves only men. Life is the Song and not the Shrine." Another Keeper of the Ancient Ways laid aside his incense and his holy book and struck him in the face. He fell once more. . . .

"What shall we do, O Grand Musician, with the Liar who hates the Shrine of Older Life?" cried the Hater still in masquerade. . . .

"He must die upon the wall. Let him suffer for his lies. Let him hang where everyone may know the nature of his ugly melodies of desecration. Hang him on the great machine of death."

SESSION GOAL	READING
To be aware of our tendencies to judge others.	Chapters XVI–XIX of *The Singer*

REFLECT

✳ Why did the Keepers of the Ancient Ways reject what the Singer said?

✳ Why do we often react negatively when we hear something we disagree with rather than listen openly?

⊰⊱ STUDY ⊱⊰

READ MARK 14:53-72.

⁵³They took Jesus to the high priest, and all the chief priests, the elders and the teachers of the law came together. ⁵⁴Peter followed him at a distance, right into the courtyard of the high priest. There he sat with the guards and warmed himself at the fire.

⁵⁵The chief priests and the whole Sanhedrin were looking for evidence against Jesus so that they could put him to death, but they did not find any. ⁵⁶Many testified falsely against him, but their statements did not agree.

⁵⁷Then some stood up and gave this false testimony against him: ⁵⁸"We heard him say, 'I will destroy this temple made with human hands and in three days will build another, not made with hands.'" ⁵⁹Yet even then their testimony did not agree.

⁶⁰Then the high priest stood up before them and asked Jesus, "Are you not going to answer? What is this testimony that these men are bringing against you?" ⁶¹But Jesus remained silent and gave no answer.

Again the high priest asked him, "Are you the Messiah, the Son of the Blessed One?"

⁶²"I am," said Jesus. "And you will see the Son of Man sitting at the right hand of the Mighty One and coming on the clouds of heaven."

⁶³The high priest tore his clothes. "Why do we need any more witnesses?" he asked. ⁶⁴"You have heard the blasphemy. What do you think?"

They all condemned him as worthy of death. ⁶⁵Then some began to spit at him; they blindfolded him, struck him with their fists, and said, "Prophesy!" And the guards took him and beat him.

⁶⁶While Peter was below in the courtyard, one of the servant girls of the high priest came by. ⁶⁷When she saw Peter warming himself, she looked closely at him.

"You also were with that Nazarene, Jesus," she said.

⁶⁸But he denied it. "I don't know or understand what you're talking about," he said, and went out into the entryway.

⁶⁹When the servant girl saw him there, she said again to those standing around, "This fellow is one of them." ⁷⁰Again he denied it.

After a little while, those standing near said to Peter, "Surely you are one of them, for you are a Galilean."

⁷¹He began to call down curses, and he swore to them, "I don't know this man you're talking about."

⁷²Immediately the rooster crowed the second time. Then Peter remembered the word Jesus had spoken to him: "Before the rooster crows twice you will disown me three times." And he broke down and wept.

1. After three years of public ministry, Jesus is secretly arrested and brought to trial in the middle of the night. How did the chief priests try to rig the proceedings against Jesus?

2. What specific accusation did the witnesses bring?

> The Ten Commandments prohibit false testimony
> (Exodus 20:16). Two or three witnesses were necessary
> for conviction. If they were proven to be lying, their
> punishment would be the same as what the accused
> would have faced if found guilty (Deuteronomy 19:15-19).

3. In the midst of the chaos of the trial, how does Jesus ironi-
   cally take control?

> The temple was a supreme symbol of Israel's
> identity and where God's very presence resided. To
> destroy it then would have been a blasphemous
> act worthy of death (see Leviticus 24:16).
>
> The accusations regarding the temple and Jesus being
> the Messiah—a king from David's line—are logically
> connected because the king was promised authority
> over the temple (2 Samuel 7:12-14; Zechariah 6:12-13).

4. Why does Jesus' answer in Mark 14:62 make the religious
   leaders react so strongly?

Jesus combines two messianic quotations—Daniel 7:13-14 (the Son of Man coming on clouds who is given authority over the nations) and Psalm 110:1 (the Messiah sitting at God's right hand). Together these paint a picture of one who would sit in judgment, restore Israel, and have dominion over the world.

5. How does Peter respond to the accusations made against him?

6. What contrasts do you see between the scene with Jesus and the scene with Peter?

7. What is Mark trying to teach us by these contrasts?

✳ Why is clearly stating that we follow Jesus sometimes hard to do?

✳ We may criticize Peter for not sufficiently heeding Jesus' warning about betraying him (Mark 14:27-31) and being so quick to cave in. Instead, how can being aware of our own weaknesses make us less judgmental and more compassionate toward others?

PRAY

Lord Jesus, thank you that your blessings flow into the cracks and brokenness of my life, that you bring forgiveness, healing, and wholeness. Thank you for the amazing faithfulness you showed during your trial, and that we can count on that same faithfulness to us. Amen.

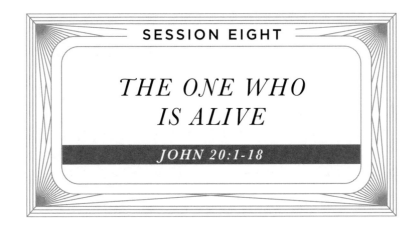

In the morning, the wreckage of the great machine lay in splintered beams beneath the wall. It had fallen in the night....

A workman finally spied the giant tension cable that drew the heavy chains. He feared to see the mutilation he would find beneath the tangled cables and the ropes....

At length he found the foreman sent to direct the clean-up operation at the wall. "Tell the Grand Musician," he said, "there is no body in the wreckage and the manacles are empty."...

The first faint coloring of dawn found her lying in fatigue, still begging for her legs which had not suffered any loss for all her worry....

She felt someone beside her on the simple mat that was her bed.

"You worried about your legs for nothing," said a voice.

She sat upright in her fear. In but a moment she was on her feet and seemed about to run. Then she looked at him more fully. Her heart was pumping. "Can it be?"

And she concluded in her madness, "It is!" She threw herself into the Singer's arms with such a strong embrace it all but knocked him over. "You're alive—alive." . . .

And those who know the Ancient Star-Song watch with singing for the sign of footprints in the galaxies through which the little planet rides in routine cycles of despair. But Joy seldom sleeps for long. And someday in a lonely moment mankind will shake an unfamiliar hand and find it wounded.

SESSION GOAL	READING
To live in the light of the resurrection.	Chapters XX-XXIV of *The Singer*

 **REFLECT**

✳ Tell about a time you were delighted by a surprise.

✳ What has helped you in times of sadness or grief?

STUDY

READ JOHN 20:1-18.

¹Early on the first day of the week, while it was still dark, Mary Magdalene went to the tomb and saw that the stone had been removed from the entrance. ²So she came running to Simon Peter and the other disciple, the one Jesus loved, and said, "They have taken the Lord out of the tomb, and we don't know where they have put him!"

³So Peter and the other disciple started for the tomb. ⁴Both were running, but the other disciple outran Peter and reached the tomb first. ⁵He bent over and looked in at the strips of linen lying there but did not go in. ⁶Then Simon Peter came along behind him and went straight into the tomb. He saw the strips of linen lying there, ⁷as well as the cloth that had been wrapped around Jesus' head. The cloth was still lying in its place, separate from the linen. ⁸Finally the other disciple, who had reached the tomb first, also went inside. He saw and believed. ⁹(They still did not understand from Scripture that Jesus had to rise from the dead.) ¹⁰Then the disciples went back to where they were staying.

¹¹Now Mary stood outside the tomb crying. As she wept, she bent over to look into the tomb ¹²and saw two angels in white, seated where Jesus' body had been, one at the head and the other at the foot.

¹³They asked her, "Woman, why are you crying?"

"They have taken my Lord away," she said, "and I don't know where they have put him." ¹⁴At this, she turned around and saw Jesus standing there, but she did not realize that it was Jesus.

¹⁵He asked her, "Woman, why are you crying? Who is it you are looking for?"

Thinking he was the gardener, she said, "Sir, if you have carried him away, tell me where you have put him, and I will get him."

¹⁶Jesus said to her, "Mary."

She turned toward him and cried out in Aramaic, "Rabboni!" (which means "Teacher").

¹⁷Jesus said, "Do not hold on to me, for I have not yet ascended to the Father. Go instead to my brothers and tell them, 'I am ascending to my Father and your Father, to my God and your God.'"

¹⁸Mary Magdalene went to the disciples with the news: "I have seen the Lord!" And she told them that he had said these things to her.

1. What is the significance that the first person to testify to the empty tomb is a woman?

2. What did Peter and the other disciple believe, and what did they still not understand?

As noted in John 11:23-24, the disciples would have been familiar with the Jewish concept of resurrection. But the idea in the first century was that all God's people would be resurrected at the end of the age. What was new was that Jesus talked about one person rising from death as a sign and promise of the general resurrection to come.

3. Why do you think Mary Magdalene remained when the other two left?

4. Why doesn't she recognize Jesus at first?

5. How does Mary react when she finally recognizes Jesus?

Verse 17 has been notoriously difficult to understand. Jesus is possibly trying to say that life is not going to be the way it was, that things will not go back to "normal." Therefore, she shouldn't hang on to him—perhaps figuratively and literally. A new reality is afoot, and he will soon be returning to the Father.

6. What is the significance of the task that Jesus gives Mary?

RESPOND

✳ How can Jesus' presence help us when we are in grief?

✳ In light of the resurrection, how have our lives changed?

PRAY

God of love, we thank you that though we were once dead in our sins, you have in your great mercy raised us to new life in Christ and seated us with him in your presence, just as he is. May we live lives that reflect this new reality, that we are new creations transformed by your power and grace. Amen.

LEADING A SMALL GROUP

LEADING A BIBLE DISCUSSION can be an enjoyable and rewarding experience. But it can also be intimidating—especially if you've never done it before. If this is how you feel, you're in good company.

Remember when God asked Moses to lead the Israelites out of Egypt? Moses replied, "Please send someone else" (Exodus 4:13)! But God gave Moses the help (human and divine) he needed to be a strong leader.

Leading a Bible discussion is not difficult if you follow certain guidelines. You don't need to be an expert on the Bible or a trained teacher. The suggestions listed below can help you to effectively fulfill your role as leader—and enjoy doing it.

PREPARING FOR THE STUDY

1. As you study the passage before the group meeting, ask God to help you understand it and apply it in your own life. Unless this happens, you will not be prepared to lead others. Pray too for the various members of the group. Ask God to open your hearts to the message of his Word and motivate you to action.

2. Read the introduction to the entire guide to get an overview of the subject at hand and the issues that will be explored.

3. Be ready to respond to the "Reflect" questions with a personal story or example. The group will be only as vulnerable and open as its leader.

4. Read the chapter of the companion book that is recommended at the beginning of the session.

5. Read and reread the assigned Bible passage to familiarize yourself with it. You may want to look up the passage in a Bible so that you can see its context.

6. This study guide is based on the New International Version of the Bible. It will help you and the group if you use this translation as the basis for your study and discussion.

7. Carefully work through each question in the study. Spend time in meditation and reflection as you consider how to respond.

8. Write your thoughts and responses in the space provided in the study guide. This will help you to express your understanding of the passage clearly.

9. It might help you to have a Bible dictionary handy. Use it to look up any unfamiliar words, names, or places.

10. Take the final (application) study questions and the "Respond" portion of each study seriously. Consider what this means for your life, what changes you may need to make in your lifestyle, or what actions you can take in your church or with people you know. Remember that the group will follow your lead in responding to the studies.

LEADING THE STUDY

1. Be sure everyone in your group has a study guide and a Bible. Encourage the group to prepare beforehand for each discussion by reading the introduction to the guide and by working through the questions for that session.

2. At the beginning of your first time together, explain that these studies are meant to be discussions, not lectures. Encourage the members of the group to participate. However, do not put pressure on those who may be hesitant to speak during the first few sessions.

3. Begin the study on time. Open with prayer, asking God to help the group understand and apply the passage.

4. Have a group member read aloud the excerpt from *The Singer* at the beginning of the discussion. This will remind the group of the topic of the study.

5. Discuss the "Reflect" questions before reading the Bible passage. These kinds of opening questions are important for several reasons. First, there is usually a stiffness that needs to be overcome before people will begin to talk openly. A good question will break the ice.

   Second, most people will have lots of different things going on in their minds (dinner, an exam, an important meeting coming up, how to get the car fixed) that have nothing to do with the study. A creative question will get their attention and draw them into the discussion.

   Third, opening questions can reveal where our thoughts or feelings need to be transformed by Scripture. That is why it is important not to read the passage before the "Reflect" questions are asked. The passage will tend to color the honest reactions people would otherwise give, because they feel they are supposed to think the way the Bible does.

6. Have a group member read aloud the Scripture passage.

7. As you ask the questions, keep in mind that they are designed to be used just as they are written. You may simply read them aloud. Or you may prefer to express them in your own words.

    There may be times when it is appropriate to deviate from the study guide. For example, a question may already have been answered. If so, move on to the next question. Or someone may raise an important question not covered in the guide. Take time to discuss it, but try to keep the group from going off on tangents.

8. Avoid offering the first answer to a study question. Repeat or rephrase questions if necessary until they are clearly understood. An eager group quickly becomes passive and silent if members think the leader will give all the *right* answers.

9. Don't be afraid of silence. People may need time to think about the question before formulating their answers.

10. Don't be content with just one answer. Ask, "What do the rest of you think?" or, "Anything else?" until several people have given answers to a question. You might point out one of the study sidebars to help spur discussion; for example, "Does the quotation on page seventeen provide any insight as you think about this question?"

11. Acknowledge all contributions. Be affirming whenever possible. Never reject an answer. If it is clearly off-base, ask, "Which verse led you to that conclusion?" or, "What do the rest of you think?"

12. Don't expect every answer to be addressed to you, even though this will probably happen at first. As group members become more at ease, they will begin to truly interact with each other. This is one sign of healthy discussion.

13. Don't be afraid of controversy. It can be stimulating! If you don't resolve an issue completely, don't be frustrated. Move on and keep it in mind for later. A subsequent study may solve the problem.

14. Try to periodically summarize what the group has said about the passage. This helps to draw together the various ideas mentioned and gives continuity to the study. But don't preach.

15. When you come to the application questions at the end of each "Study" section, be willing to keep the discussion going by describing how you have been affected by the study. It's important that we each apply the message of the passage to ourselves in a specific way.

    Depending on the makeup of your group and the length of time you've been together, you may or may not want to discuss the "Respond" section. If not, allow the group to read it and reflect on it silently. Encourage members to make specific commitments and to write them in their study guide. Ask them the following week how they did with their commitments.

16. Conclude your time together with conversational prayer. Ask for God's help in following through on the commitments you've made.

17. End the group discussion on time.

Many more suggestions and helps are found in The Big Book on Small Groups *by Jeffrey Arnold.*

IVP SIGNATURE BIBLE STUDIES

As companions to the IVP Signature Collection, IVP Signature Bible Studies feature the inductive study method, equipping individuals and groups to explore the biblical truths embedded in these books.

Basic Christianity Bible Study
JOHN STOTT

How to Give Away Your Faith Bible Study
PAUL E. LITTLE

The Singer Bible Study, CALVIN MILLER

Knowing God Bible Study, J. I. PACKER

A Long Obedience in the Same Direction Bible Study, EUGENE H. PETERSON

Good News About Injustice Bible Study
GARY A. HAUGEN

Hearing God Bible Study
DALLAS WILLARD

The Heart of Racial Justice Bible Study
BRENDA SALTER McNEIL AND
RICK RICHARDSON

True Story Bible Study, JAMES CHOUNG

The Next Worship Bible Study
SANDRA MARIA VAN OPSTAL

Jesus Through Middle Eastern Eyes Bible Study, KENNETH E. BAILEY

Strong and Weak Bible Study
ANDY CROUCH